The Three Little Rabbits

Written and illustrated by Mandy Stanley

Collins

2

4

6

8

Help!

9

11

12

Three rabbits, three houses

straw

wood

bricks

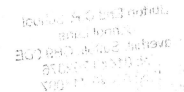

Ideas for reading

Written by Clare Dowdall, PhD
Lecturer and Primary Literacy Consultant

Learning objectives: children read and understand simple sentences; they talk about the features of their own environment and how environments might vary from one another; they safely use and explore a variety of materials, tools and techniques

Curriculum links: Expressive arts and design: Being imaginative

High frequency words: the, and, no, you

Interest words: hungry, blow, ha ha!

Resources: high frequency word flashcards, junk modelling material

Word count: 35

Getting started

- Look at the front cover and read the title together. Look carefully at the illustration. Ask children to describe each rabbit and what it is holding. Help them with vocabulary to support language development.

- Turn to the blurb. Model how to read the speech bubble, using your finger to point to each word, and use appropriate expression. Ask children to tell you about the character who is speaking, and introduce the term *speech bubble* to describe how the wolf's words are presented.

- Ask children to suggest what is going to happen to the rabbits and the wolf in this story, and whether this story sounds like another well-known story.

- Practise reading the high frequency words using flashcards. Help children to notice tricky parts of the words, and to read them accurately.

Reading and responding

- Model reading pp2–5. After reading the text, discuss what is happening on each page and ask children to suggest what the rabbits might be thinking and feeling.